Croc and Ally

For my second-grade teacher,
Jeannine Block. I wrote my first story in
her creative writing class and have never
been the same since—DA

PENGUIN WORKSHOP
An imprint of Penguin Random House LLC, New York

First published simultaneously in paperback and hardcover in the United States of America by
Penguin Workshop, an imprint of Penguin Random House LLC, New York, 2022

Visit us online at penguinrandomhouse.com.

Library of Congress Cataloging-in-Publication Data is available.

Manufactured in China

ISBN 9780593387627 (hc)   10 9 8 7 6 5 4 3 2 1 TOPL

Design by Julia Rosenfeld

Croc and Ally

The Best in the World

by Derek Anderson

Penguin Workshop

Ally Has Spots

"What is wrong?" asked Croc.

"I have spots!" said Ally.

"I know," said Croc.

"Quick, help me wash them off!"

cried Ally.

"Your spots will not wash off,"

said Croc.

"You have always had spots.

You will always have spots.

They are part of you."

"But I do not want spots," said Ally.

"*You* do not have spots."

"You are right," said Croc.

"We are different.

You may not like your spots,

but I do."

"There is only one way I will be happy with my spots," said Ally.

"What is that?" asked Croc.

"You are a good friend, Croc," said Ally.

"I know, I know," said Croc.

Ally Is Ready!

"What in the world are you doing?"

asked Croc.

"I am getting ready," said Ally.

"What are you getting ready for?"

asked Croc.

"Anything," said Ally.

"Somebody saw a giant bee

in the swamp.

It can't sting me in this armor."

"I have a flashlight

in case the sun goes out."

"And this umbrella will protect me

if a star falls out of the sky,"

said Ally.

"It is good to be safe," said Croc.

"But you don't have to be afraid

of everything."

"I am *ready* for anything,"

said Ally.

"I am hungry," said Croc.

"I am ready for lunch.

See you later."

"Wait for me!" said Ally.

The Best in the World

"What are you watching?"

asked Croc.

"A video of a frog," said Ally.

"She is the best in the world

at hopping."

"Wow, she can hop!" said Croc.

"I want to be the best in the world at something," said Ally.

"What will you be the best at?"

asked Croc.

"I won't know until I try," said Ally.

"I will make a video of you,"

said Croc.

Ally tried jumping high.

He tried lifting something heavy.

He tried standing on his head.

He tried standing on his feet.

"I am not the best in the world at anything," said Ally.

"That is not true," said Croc.

"You are the best in the world at being Ally."

"I am?" said Ally.

"Yes. There is no one else that is exactly like you," said Croc.

"I am the best in the world!"

said Ally.